KU-305-629

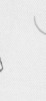

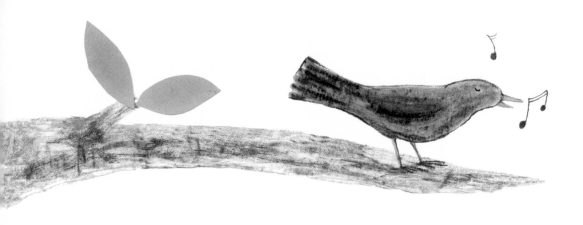

First published in 2011 by Child's Play (International) Ltd
Ashworth Road, Bridgemead, Swindon SN5 7YD

Published in USA by Child's Play Inc
250 Minot Avenue, Auburn, Maine 04210

Distributed in Australia by Child's Play Australia Pty Ltd
Unit 10/20 Narabang Way
Belrose, NSW 2085

Text and illustrations copyright © 2011 Carol Thompson
The moral right of the author/illustrator has been asserted

All rights reserved

ISBN 978-1-84643-575-1

L170812CPL11125751

Printed and bound in Heshan, China

1 3 5 7 9 10 8 6 4 2

A catalogue record of this book is available from the British Library

www.childs-play.com

SNUG

Carol Thompson

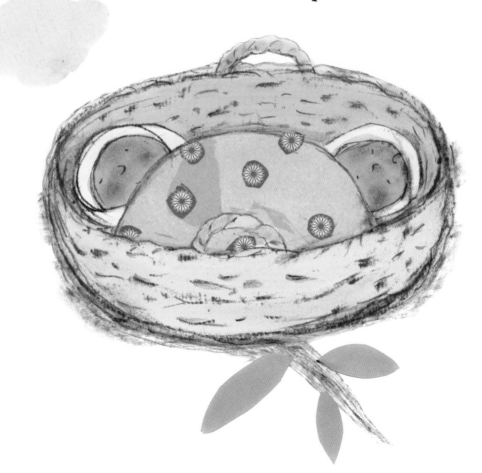

As snug as a bug
in a very old rug,

Snug as a mole
in his underground hole.

Snug is a bulb deep under snow,
Snug is the earthworm curled up below.

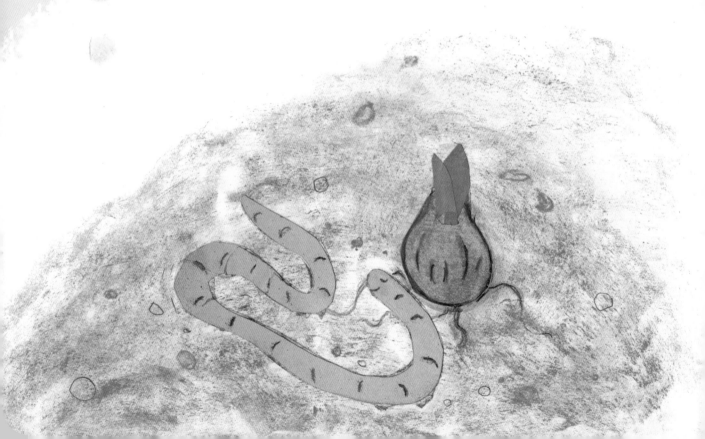

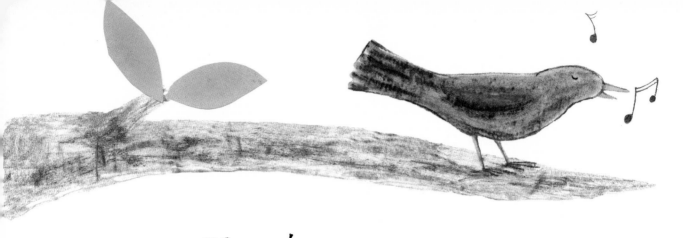

As snug as a bird in a feathery nest,

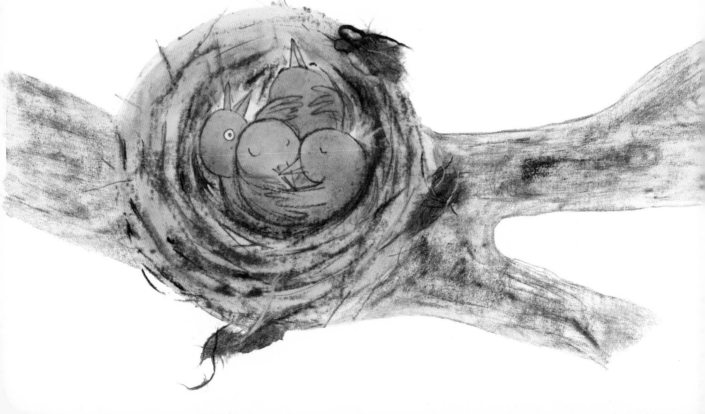

Snug is a piglet
wearing her vest.

Does a slug feel snug
asleep in the mud?

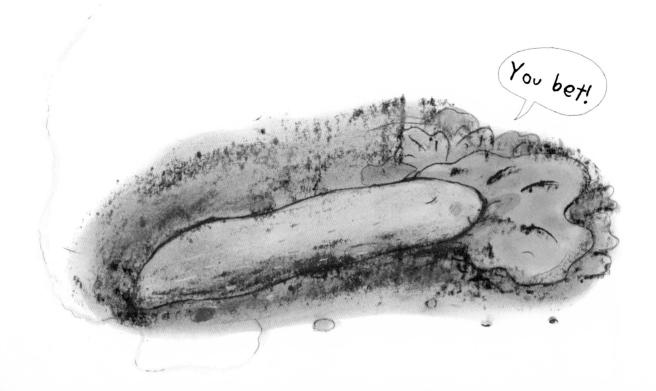

A squash
and a squeeze!

As snug as
green peas.

A snug
little snail,
curled head
to its tail,

A snuggled down mouse
in his very own house.

As snug as a fox
in hand-knitted socks,

As snug as a cat
curled up on a mat.

As snug
as a hug...

A hug is
SO snug!